For Alex and her pet snowball, Horsey, and for
Wednesday—best pet ever —M.H.

For my not-at-all normal parents, and for Pia and Izzy,
who, I hope, think I'm not at all normal either, and for
my good old stinky embarrassing pet, Olive —G.P.

Text copyright © 2012 by Matthea Harvey
Illustrations copyright © 2012 by Giselle Potter

All rights reserved. Published in the United States by Schwartz & Wade Books, an imprint of
Random House Children's Books, a division of Random House, Inc., New York.
Schwartz & Wade Books and the colophon are trademarks of Random House, Inc.
Visit us on the Web! randomhouse.com/kids
Educators and librarians, for a variety of teaching tools, visit us at randomhouse.com/teachers

Library of Congress Cataloging-in-Publication Data
Harvey, Matthea.
Cecil the pet glacier / Matthea Harvey ; illustrated by Giselle Potter.—1st ed.
p. cm.
Summary: Ruby Small's embarrassingly eccentric parents take her on a vacation to Norway where she
acquires an unwanted pet, a glacier named Cecil, who finds a way to melt Ruby's heart.
ISBN 978-0-375-86773-6 (trade) — ISBN 978-0-375-96773-3 (glb)
[1. Pets—Fiction. 2. Glaciers—Fiction. 3. Eccentrics and eccentricities—Fiction. 4. Norway—Fiction.]
I. Potter, Giselle, ill. II. Title.
PZ7.H2678Ce 2012
[Fic]—dc23
2011018657

The text of this book is set in Archetype.
The illustrations were rendered in watercolor.
MANUFACTURED IN CHINA
10 9 8 7 6 5 4 3 2 1

First Edition

Cecil

THE PET GLACIER

MATTHEA HARVEY

Illustrated by
GISELLE POTTER

schwartz & wade books · new york

Ruby Small was a normal little girl.

Perhaps that was to make up for having two not-normal-at-all parents. Ruby lived in a yellow-and-pink-striped house with a chimney that was so close to sky-blue that on some days it was invisible. Outside was a sign that read TOPIARY & TIARAS: SPRIGS & SPARKLES. Mr. Small was a topiary gardener: he trimmed trees into animal shapes—oaks became owls, pines became platypuses, maples became marsupials, and hedges became hedgehogs. Mrs. Small was a tiara designer.

On summer evenings, Mrs. Small would put on her fanciest tiara and Mr. Small would set up the record player, and the two would tango cheek to cheek among the topiary.

TOPIARY & TIARAS: SPRIGS & SPARKLES

Inside, Ruby would pray that no one from school would walk by. She'd pull the curtains shut and serve milk and bran muffins to The Three Jennifers, her identical dolls, who were dressed like her in brown pinafores, plain black headbands, and brown shoes with the shoelaces triple-knotted.

"So, Hedgeling," said Mr. Small one day. "Where would you like to go on vacation this year? In China, there is a miniature topiary herb garden I've always wanted to visit. They have a tiny rhinoceros made out of rosemary."

"No way," muttered Ruby grumpily.

"Norway! What a fabulous idea!" said Mrs. Small.

Ruby knew there was no point in arguing.

By the time vacation rolled around, the shrubs had stopped growing and Mr. Small was anxious to leave. He moped, sadly snipping at the air. One day he even trimmed a huge hairy crocodile into his beard.

Mrs. Small piled fifteen hatboxes into the car— she didn't like to repeat tiaras even on vacation— and they were off.

Ruby was in charge of the passports, of course. On the plane, she stared at the photographs inside while her parents drank milk-and-Cokes (their favorite invented drink) and played miniature Ping-Pong on their foldout trays.

Really, Ruby thought, it was hard to believe she was related to these people. Sometimes she felt so lonely, even with The Three Jennifers.

"Mama? Papa?" said Ruby.

"Yes?" they answered as the tiny Ping-Pong ball hit the passenger in front of them.

"When we get back, do you think I could get a pet?"

"Why, darling, of course!" said Mrs. Small. "I've always thought a tank of moon medusas, those glow-in-the-dark jellyfish, would be beautiful in the living room. We could eat TV dinners in front of them."

"Or," said Mr. Small, "I have a friend who is thinking of getting rid of his flea circus. Apparently the little fellas are terrific at soccer."

"I was thinking of something a bit cuddlier," said Ruby. "Like a dog."

Mr. and Mrs. Small looked puzzled.

That first morning at the guesthouse in Horfensnufen, breakfast was four tiny fish on a piece of toast, or, in her parents' case, a piece of toast on four tiny fish—they loved eating food upside down.

Afterward, the Smalls walked to the tourist office. "Welcome, Smalls," a blue-haired man named Sven said severely. "Today, glacier."

The Smalls followed Sven outside
to a fleet of pink snowmobiles.
"Little Small, you ride with me,"
said Sven. "Big Smalls, saddle up,
as they say in the American movies."

After seventy minutes (or one
hour and ten minutes), Sven slowed
to a stop. "There are several glaciers
near Horfensnufen, but this one,
Cecilsmater, is the most beautiful
of all. Today it is calving."

"Calving?" asked Ruby.

"Yes," said Sven. "When glaciers get too big, littler glaciers break off and float down the river. It is like a cow having a baby calf."

Ruby looked in the water, where several little glaciers floated downstream. Some were as big as paddleboats. Others were small. Ruby thought a tiny, strange-shaped one seemed to be approaching them.

The little glacier slid down the hill
and came to a stop at Ruby's ankle. Ruby
moved away. The little glacier followed.

Ruby hid behind her mother.
The glacier hid behind Ruby.

"Why, Ruby, it seems you've found
yourself a little ice-pet!" said Mr. Small
delightedly.

Ruby and The Three Jennifers looked
down at the lump with dismay. "Oh no,"
said Ruby. "Please no."

Sure enough, when Sven and the Smalls got back onto their snowmobiles, the little glacier followed.

Back at the tourist office, Mrs. Small said, "I think your pet needs a name."

"It's not my pet," said Ruby. "It's just a piece of ice."

"Little Small, call glacier Cecil," said Sven, and walked into his office and shut the door.

From then on, Cecil was always at Ruby's ankle. She began to count the days until they could return home and leave the ice-pest behind.

On their last night, Mr. Small came back to the room with a red cooler and a big smile.

"Are we having a picnic on the plane?" Ruby asked hopefully.

"No, Hedgeling, this is for Cecil."

"But I don't want him to come with us," said Ruby.

"Darling," said Mrs. Small, "you wanted a pet, and a pet has found you. And he sparkles like a diamond! You couldn't have found a more delightful pet if you'd dreamed him up."

Ruby scowled.

At the airport, Ruby prayed that the baggage inspectors would not let Cecil leave the country. But Cecil sailed right through the X-ray machine.

Back at home, the Smalls discovered that a pet glacier has special needs. For one thing, Cecil ate pebbles. Every night the Smalls would put a plate of pebbles on the floor and Cecil would glide over it and absorb them. Finicky like a cat, he liked white and black pebbles but wouldn't eat the gray ones. He didn't speak, but when he was happy he creaked.

110 S. Elm St., Box 299
Waterman, IL 60556

Because Cecil was made of very hard ice, he could make it through a sunny day. But every night he needed to be watered with ice water, then put in the red cooler. Rain was bad for him because it was never cold enough and it made him melt. Once a week, Mrs. Small would turn Cecil upside down and groom him. Often he'd have picked up trash from the road—a soda can, a branch, a lottery ticket, chewed gum.

But Ruby had no interest in her pet. On weekends, she and The Three Jennifers would go into their room and lock Cecil out. He would nudge the door, leaving a wet patch below the doorknob. After a bit, he would slide sadly back to his cooler.

On weekdays, Cecil would follow Ruby to school and wait
for her in the bushes. At recess, he would peer through the
fence at Ruby and The Three Jennifers playing in a corner
alone. Once, to tease Ruby, two mean boys tangoed past her,
making a small tear run down her cheek. Cecil shed a tear
then too, from the area where his eyes would have been if
he'd had eyes, which he didn't.

One recess, Ruby's class was deep into a game of four square when a lightning storm hit. Miss Smith, Ruby's teacher, hurried the children inside, then looked around the playground. In a hidden corner, Ruby was carefully putting raincoats on The Three Jennifers.

Miss Smith charged over, grabbed Ruby's hand, and hurried her into the classroom. In the commotion, Ruby dropped one of The Three Jennifers into the mud. "Wait!" she cried, but Miss Smith had already shut the door behind them.

As Miss Smith was toweling off the class, Ruby stood by the window and watched the rain wash The Jennifer away. Ruby burst into loud sobs.

Then, out of the corner of her eye, she saw a small white lump. It was Cecil, moving back and forth across the playground. As the rain pelted him, he grew smaller and smaller, until Ruby thought he'd disappeared entirely.

Just as geography was about to begin, there was
a thumping at the door. Miss Smith opened it and the
class craned their necks to see, in the doorway, a very
small piece of ice with a Jennifer sticking out of it.
"Cecil!" cried Ruby. "You found her! Oh, Cecil!"

The class looked at Ruby in amazement. Then, "Help! I need some ice water and a plate of pebbles!" she cried with such authority that two of her classmates did as they were told.

Ruby watered Cecil, watched him move weakly across the plate of pebbles, and put him in the cafeteria freezer.

Only then did she change The Jennifer's soaked clothes.

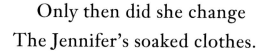

Later that afternoon, Cecil was allowed to sit next to Ruby in class. After math, a quiet boy named Murphy, who often read books at recess, came over and asked, "Can I pet him?"

Ruby looked up, startled. "Well, he's very cold. You'll have to get a mitten or something."

Murphy took one of the towels, wrapped it around his hand, and stroked Cecil's back. "What a wonderful pet," he said. "I've never seen anything like him."

Ruby smiled. "He is pretty unusual, isn't he?"

Cecil creaked more than he had ever creaked before.

After school let out, two children (walking), three dolls (riding),
and one glacier (sliding) went home to the Smalls' house.

As she walked through the garden, Ruby picked up a pair of scissors and handed them to her father, who was in a tree, trying to perfect a penguin.

Then she knocked on her mother's studio door. "Mama?" she asked. "Yes, Ruby?" replied Mrs. Small.

SPARKLES

"If you wanted to make a tiara for Cecil," said Ruby, "I don't think he'd mind."